Messages

Pat Thomson
and Caroline Crossland

Collins

This edition produced for The Book People Ltd
Hall Wood Avenue, Haydock
St Helens WA11 9UL

Published by A & C Black in 1992
Published by Collins in 1993
10 9 8 7 6
Collins an imprint of HarperCollins*Publishers* Ltd,
77-85 Fulham Palace Road, Hammersmith, London W6 8JB.

ISBN 0 00 763094 8

Text © Pat Thomson 1992
Illustrations © Caroline Crossland 1992

The Great Idea

When Jo came downstairs
that Friday morning,
his mother had left
him a note as usual.
She worked on the
local newspaper
and often went
out early and
came home late.

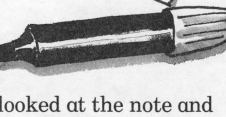

Jo looked at the note and
took out his marker-pen.
It was the one he kept
for changing things.
He changed a few
words in Mum's
note.

He picked up his lunch and PE kit and hurried out. He kept his marker handy. When he got to the end of the road, he knew he would need it again.

He couldn't leave it like that.

Alison lived down
by the park and
he called for her
on most days.

While he was
waiting, he
walked over
to the swings.

NO PERSONS OVER
10 YEARS OF AGE
ALLOWED ON SWINGS

There was always something to do in the park.

NO PERSONS OVER
100 YEARS OF AGE
ALLOWED ON SWINGS

Stop writing on things, Jo. You'll get into trouble.

I'm not doing anything. It's interesting.

They called for Amina who lived next door to Alison, and walked on to school.

Alison was worried about people who were unkind to animals. Amina wanted to protect children from bullies. That gave Jo an idea.

He wanted his friend Spud to join, too,
and Alison and Amina agreed.

In the playground, Jo found Spud sitting behind the dustbins. He was reading a comic. Jo sat down beside him and spoke in a low voice.

Spud was interested. He liked doing secret things. They drew a badge and planned to make four of them in the art class.

They also made up
a secret sign
and signalled to
Alison and Amina.

What are they doing?

No idea.

Towards the end of afternoon school, a paper aeroplane flew across the room.

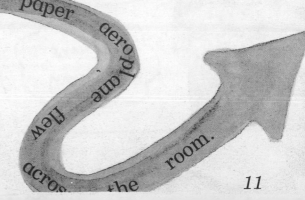

11

It landed on Jo's desk and he undid
it carefully.

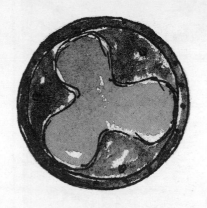

Jo hurried home. He was so full of ideas for the new society, he only stopped once. He saw a manhole cover.

He couldn't pass it by.

Jo let himself into the house. He changed his clothes and scrubbed at his fingers.

He never seemed to quite get rid of the marker ink.

Then he went to the refrigerator to get his tea. He would just have time to watch one TV programme before he went round to Alison's. Tonight was the first meeting of The Protectors.

The Protectors

At six o'clock, the telephone rang.

Jo locked the door behind him and ran down the path. He took a short cut across the playing field and squeezed through the hedge. There was a big house on the other side.

Jo stopped and looked at the gate. He had never really noticed the sign before. How had he missed it? He took out his marker.

He ran the rest of the way to
Alison's house. He opened the gate
and went straight to the shed.

He was neatly underlining
the notice when Amina
opened the door and
he fell in.

PRIVATE
Danger
KEEP
OUT
Death Rays
working

Alison had brought some stools and, on the bench, there were four mugs and some orange juice. Alison was pouring some juice when they heard three loud, slow knocks.

Amina opened the door and Spud
bounced in, carrying
the four badges.
The girls pinned
theirs on their
cardigans. Jo pinned
his on his T-shirt.
Spud pinned his on himself.

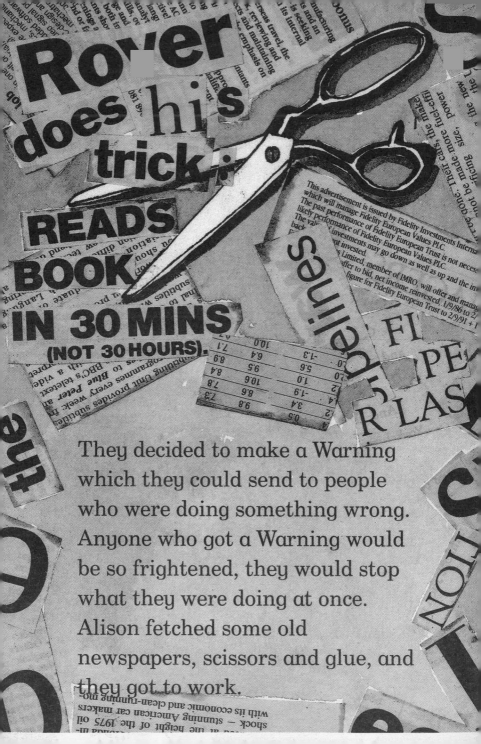

They decided to make a Warning which they could send to people who were doing something wrong. Anyone who got a Warning would be so frightened, they would stop what they were doing at once. Alison fetched some old newspapers, scissors and glue, and they got to work.

Bad news on the gnome front

The Warning took longer to make than they had thought. It was hard to find the right letters and cut them out. They kept the message as short as possible and wrote *The Protectors* in felt pen to save time. Spud drew a dagger, dripping with blood, to make it more frightening.

They realised they would need a lot of Warnings. This was a blow. It had taken a long time to do just one.

Then they got down to the serious business. Who were they going to protect? Alison was the first to speak.

She was very unhappy about the animals in cages. The others had ideas, too. Spud knew a big house on the edge of town where a dog was always howling behind a wall. Amina told them about a poor dog that was so fat, it could hardly walk.

Jo took out his marker-pen and notebook, and made a list.

Jo Lister
14 Rose Ave.
Hatton
Northants
U.K.
The World
The Universe.

The Protectors
1. Check pet shop.
2. Check Edgewood Hall.
3. Find out who owns fat dog.

By this time, it was getting late.

That should be enough for one week-end.

We'll start tomorrow. Meet at the pet shop at nine o'clock.

Kindness to Animals

When Jo got up on Saturday morning, there was a note from Mum.

Jo,
Had to go back to finish something. See you for lunch.
Mum xx

He ate his breakfast quickly and reached the high street before the others. The man was just opening the pet shop. Jo looked at the animals. They were all clean and lively.

He decided to question the owner.

The Protectors had only just come
into the shop, but the man looked
so cross, they turned and ran.

Jo looked in his notebook, and they decided to fetch their bikes and go out to Edgewood Hall.

EDGEWOOD HALL
Open Thursdays

When they arrived, there was no howling dog. The gates were locked. Alison and Amina tried to lift Spud up to see over the wall, but it was too high.

Jo was fingering his marker-pen
and looking at the house sign.

They decided to put a Warning
through the letter box and hope
that would do the trick.
Alison was a bit disappointed, but
there was still the lady with the
poor fat dog.

Amina had seen her in the library
on Saturdays, so they pedalled back
into town. Sure enough, the dog was
tied up outside the library.

They went into the library to look
for the owner. Jo saw a tempting
notice on the front desk.

He took out his marker.

Alison pointed to a very large lady. They were just wondering how to tackle her when they heard a voice behind them.

They dashed out of the door before
anything more could be said.
Alison and Amina were furious.

All they could do was to tuck a
Warning into the dog's collar.
The Protectors' first jobs had been
a complete disaster.

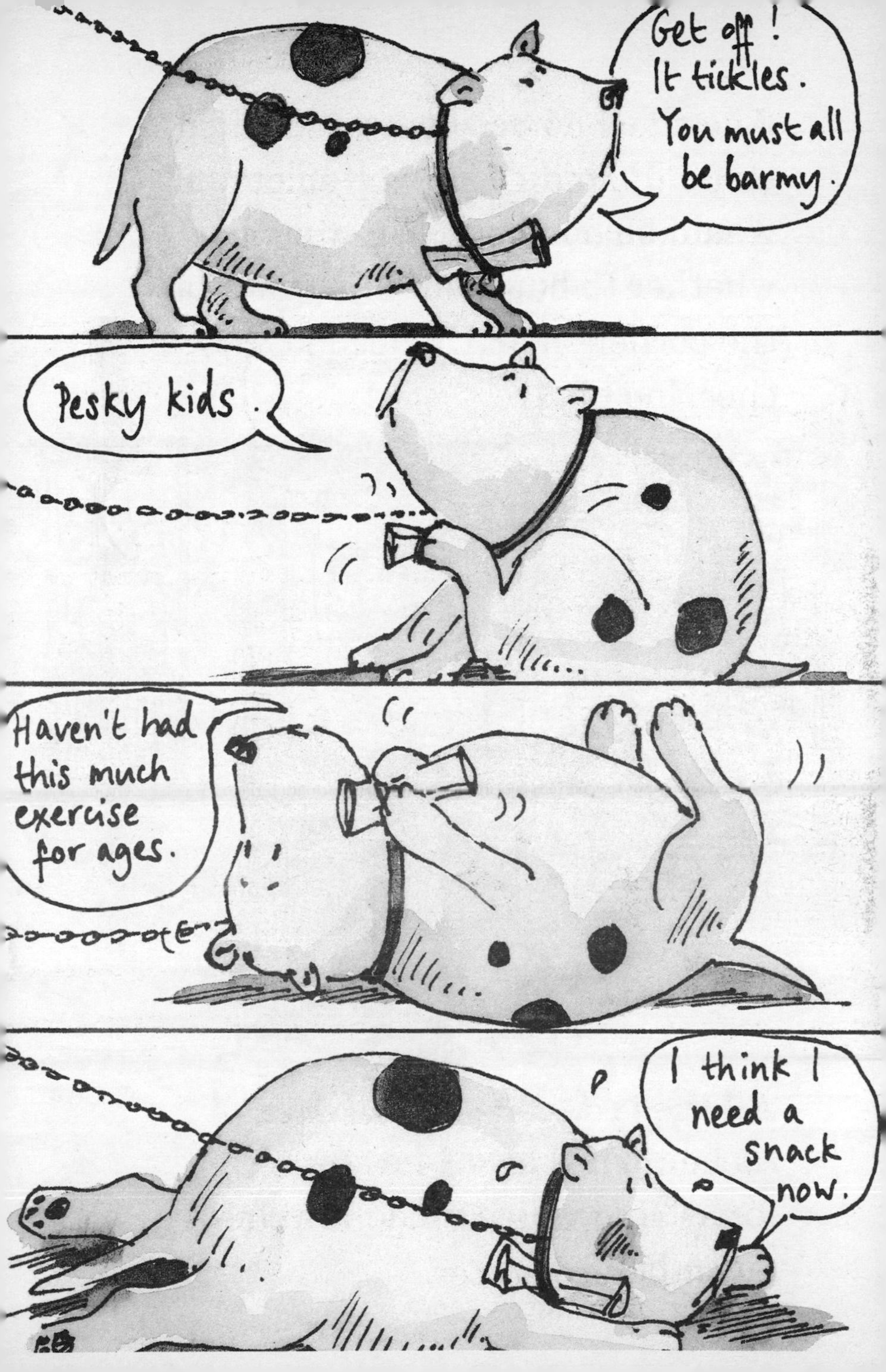
Get off! It tickles. You must all be barmy.
Pesky kids.
Haven't had this much exercise for ages.
I think I need a snack now.

Jo walked home slowly, kicking a stone. He didn't know if his mum would be home yet. He wondered whether to buy something nice at the corner shop. He needed cheering up.

As he turned away, he saw something which made him feel much better.

He cheered up at once. He took out
his marker-pen and got to work.

Suddenly he had a creepy feeling
that he was being watched.

A boy with a pale face was looking at him. The boy struggled desperately with the window but he couldn't open it. He must be locked in. He beckoned to Jo.

But as Jo started to cross the road, he saw a man come into the room. The boy moved quickly away from the window. Jo ran off, but he was planning what to write in his notebook.

7 Neathbridge Street.
Strange boy.
Never seen him before.
Looks pale.
Seems shut in.
Tried to talk to me but couldn't.
Is he a prisoner?
This could be a case for The Protectors!

The Prisoner

Jo was late on Monday morning so
he didn't see Alison before school.
He tried to speak to her after
assembly.

Alison blamed Jo for Saturday. She sent him another paper aeroplane.

You are stupid. Stop writing on things and getting us into trouble.

Miss Potter was watching so he replied on his ruler.

I don't write on things much.

At break, he was glad to have
something interesting to tell the
others. They went to a quiet place.

It sounded suspicious. Amina knew
the family who owned the shop in
Neathbridge Street so they decided
that she and Alison would go
and talk to them.

Jo and Spud could have a look at
the back of the boy's house. They
planned to go straight after school.

To keep it secret,

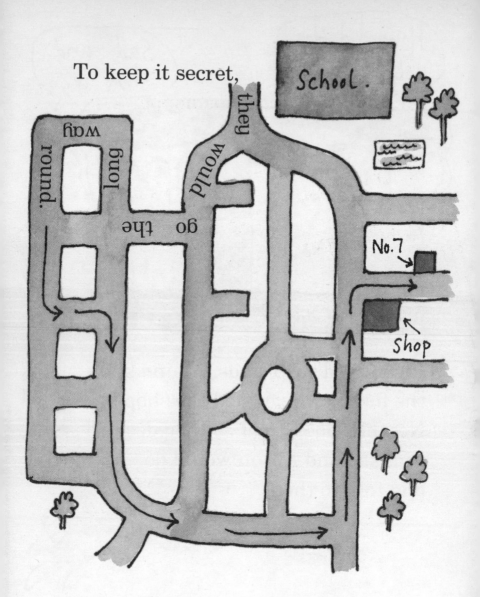

When they all met again, they were very worried. They wrote everything down.

There was plenty of evidence that something strange was happening.

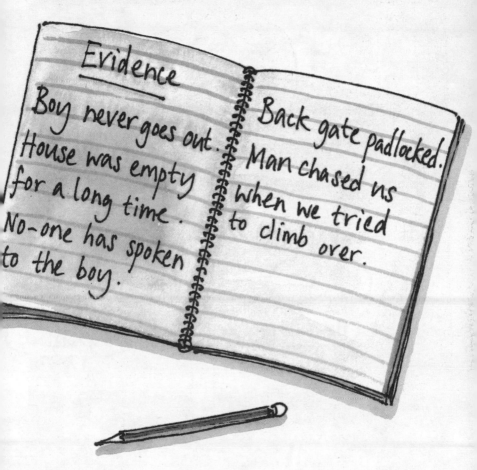

Evidence

Boy never goes out.
House was empty
for a long time.
No-one has spoken
to the boy.

Back gate padlocked.
Man chased us
when we tried
to climb over.

Perhaps the boy was in danger. They all agreed that they must make contact with him quickly.

It was all up to Jo.

When the others went home, Jo went back to the house. The boy was at the window again. Jo crossed the road and stood by the low garden wall. He held up his notebook. He had written a message on it in big writing.

The boy struggled with the window again and then shook his head.

The boy looked startled and then nodded.

The boy looked quite different now, more hopeful. For the first time, he smiled. He nodded and held up his thumbs. Jo quickly took out his marker-pen and scribbled another message.

The boy looked back over his shoulder. Jo heard a slight noise.

The man stood on the doorstep looking at Jo and his notices. He started to come down the path. Jo ran.

He arrived home out of breath. He went to get a drink and saw another note from mum.

Jo,
    Sorry. Had to go back again. Will DEFINITELY see you tomorrow. Hope you're not too bored,
            Mum xx

That was when he realised that he
had dropped his notebook!
If the man picked it up,
he would discover
everything about
The Protectors!

Found Out

On Tuesday morning, a letter
arrived for Jo's mum. Jo could tell
where it came from.

Mum read it and handed it to Jo.

Mum didn't say much but she
didn't look too pleased.

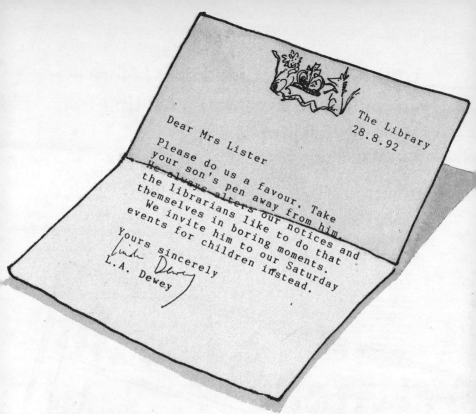

The Library
28.8.92

Dear Mrs Lister

Please do us a favour. Take
your son's pen away from him.
He always alters our notices and
the librarians like to do that
themselves in boring moments.
We invite him to our Saturday
events for children instead.

Yours sincerely
L. A. Dewey

On Wednesday, a postcard came
from the man in the pet shop.

P O S T   C A R D

Why not buy your
son a pet? It might
keep him busy and
stop him bothering
me. In my opinion,
all kids are barmy.

P.E. Turner.

Mrs. Lister,
14 Rose Avenue,
Hatton,
Northants.

Unfortunately, Mum saw it before
Jo could whisk it away. This time
Mum had plenty to say.
Jo wondered if he should tell her
about the boy.

On Thursday, the local paper
came.

Hatton Gazette

"Aliens are bugging my dog"

Mrs Cath Lawson of Arden Way fears for her dog.

Comfy Cath found a bugging device on big Edward's collar.
"I only left him for minutes," she
claimed, "and
they

got at him. I'm afraid he may be kidnapped and taken to another planet."
The cheery dog lover has put Ed on a fitness diet so he can fight bac
"Woof!" says Ed.

When Jo looked at it, he had a sinking feeling in his stomach. His mum must have seen the story on the front page.

That night, there was a note from mum.

Jo,
    Must have a serious talk with you about all these messages.
    Mum xx.

Jo knew he would have to tell her everything, but the most important thing was to help the boy. He had been past the house several times but it seemed that the boy wasn't even allowed to come to the window any more.

On Friday morning, the local radio had picked up the alien story.

He was glad his mother hadn't heard that. It was time to do something. He would have to tell the others what had happened and ask them to help rescue the boy.

When Jo came home from school that night, there was an envelope addressed to him. He opened it.

INVITATION TO
Jo and friends
PLEASE COME TO MY PARTY ON
May 12th
AT
7 Neathbridge Street
AT
2 . 30
FROM
Peter
P.T.O.

He turned the invitation over.

We've just moved here. Your mum works with my dad. I've been ill but I'm getting better now, so please bring everyone to my party.

From Peter.

P.S. Dad thinks you are the aliens. He laughed his head off.

On Saturday, Jo was woken up by the doorbell. He heard his mother open the door and went to the window to see who was there. A large van stood outside.

His mother was talking to someone. Was everyone coming to complain about him? He stayed in his room until he heard the van drive away.

Mum was smiling! She seemed pleased about something.

It's my new word processor. You're going to see a lot more of me in future.

Mum explained that from now on, her office would be at home. Her machine was linked to the ones at work.

She was so pleased, she was not as angry with Jo as he had thought she would be, but she was very stern about the marker-pen writing.

She also gave him his notebook back. Peter's father had told her all about The Protectors. He said it had cheered Peter up and he wanted to meet them all.

Jo began to feel very happy.
Mum would be at home much more.
The Protectors could become
newspaper reporters.

They could still
try to right
wrongs.

Then there was the party! He took his marker-pen and put it next to the word processor. It could stay there. He didn't need it now.

He had a lot to tell them.
Things were not so bad after all.